Herman and Marguerite
An Earth Story

Jay O'Callahan

Illustrated by Laura O'Callahan

PEACHTREE
ATLANTA

For my mother's never-ending hugs, tears, and laughter.
—*Laura O'Callahan*

For Linda, whose gift is bringing out the best.
—*Jay O'Callahan*

Special thanks to
Carolee Brockmann, Lyn Hoopes, Doug Lipman, Christine Shumock,
the South River School in Marshfield, Massachusetts,
Callaway Gardens, and the Montessori School in Scituate.

Published by
PEACHTREE PUBLISHERS, LTD.
494 Armour Circle NE
Atlanta, Georgia 30324

Text © 1996 by Jay O'Callahan
Illustrations © 1996 by Laura O'Callahan

Design by Nicola Simmons Carter and Loraine M. Balcsik

Manufactured in China
10 9 8 7 6 5 4 3 2 1

Library of Congress Cataloguing-in-Publication Data

O'Callahan, Jay.
   Herman and Marguerite: an earth story/by Jay O'Callahan: illustrations by Laura
O'Callahan.
       p.   cm.
   Summary: An earthworm and a caterpillar become friends and work together to bring a
neglected orchard back to life.
   ISBN 1-56145-103-7
   [1. Worms–Fiction. 2. Caterpillars–Fiction. 3. Friendship–Fiction.]
I. O'Callahan, Laura, ill.   II. Title.
PZ7.0184He 1996
              [E]–dc20   94-47561
                                                                          CIP
                                                                          AC

When I was a little boy,
I loved
orchards.

One day,
I wandered into an orchard
where there were no bees,
no butterflies,
no apples.
No sounds!

It was *lonely*.

Up in a lonely orchard,
everything was still.

But *underneath...*

…in the dark, crumbly earth, Herman the worm was making a tunnel. The earth felt cool and tingly. Herman loved tunneling. He squirmed by a millipede, squiggled past a roly-poly, and slithered by a snoring slug.

"Grandfather's right," he thought. "This place has got the buzz of life on it!"

Herman remembered his grandfather warning him not to go above during the day because the sun would dry him out. "Besides," Grandfather had said, "the only thing up there is a lonely orchard. It never grows apples—kinda sad."

But Herman was curious. So upward he squiggled until he poked his head up into the grass and pulled himself out of the cool, damp earth.

The sun poured down.

"Orchard," Herman called.
His tiny voice frightened him. He squirmed on.
"I'm getting so dry," he worried.

He crawled onto a little pile of stones.
The sun scorched him.
The stones baked him.
"I can't breathe!"

Shhhp. Shhhp.
Something was jiggling the stones.
It moved closer.
Something sharp jabbed him.
"Yikes!" Herman cried.

He tumbled down the stones.
Shhhp. Shhhp.
The creature came closer
and closer!
"Help!"
Herman
squeaked.

"Don't be scared. You are in the shade of a mushroom now. I'm Marguerite, the caterpillar. Who are you?"

"Herman, the worm. You're horrible and prickly!" Herman gasped.

"Those were my sharp hairs. I saw you were in trouble and I poked you to scare you out of the sun. My feet never moved so fast."

"You have feet?"

"Sure."

"What else do you have, Marguerite?"

"Well, I have eyes," she replied.

"You have everything, don't you, Marguerite?"

"I suppose."

Then Herman said, "I don't like it up here. It's too quiet."

"I know," said Marguerite, "the orchard cries at night. It needs company. It especially misses the bees buzzing around."

"Now that gives me an idea," said Marguerite as she took a blade of grass in her feet. "This place needs some fun!" She blew on the blade like a trumpet and sang a chomping song.

"CHOMP-CHOMP.
CHOMPA-CHOMPA-CHOMP-CHOMP."

She strummed and drummed and stomped and chomped.

"Sing with me, Herman!"

Herman stiffened.
"I can't sing," he mumbled shyly.
He was sure she would laugh.

Herman was so embarrassed, he tunneled straight
down into the earth. He curled into a tiny ball and
wouldn't move. His grandfather came
looking for him.
"What's the trouble, Herman?"

Herman hid his head under a crumpled leaf.
"I went above. The sun almost got me! I was
saved by a dogerpillar."
"CATerpillar,"
Grandfather smiled.

"Yes, and her name is Marguerite!"

"Well, you learned something, and you made a friend."

"I learned I'm just a dumb old worm," Herman burst out. "We don't have eyes or feet. Worms can't do any-thing!"

"What, what, what!" Grandfather sputtered. "What do you do all day?"

"I make tunnels," Herman complained.

"That's right. Nothing grows without our help."

"Really?"

"Yes. All these roots are bottoms of tops that need air and water to grow."

"I didn't know that."

"Everyone has a gift, Herman. And when we use our gifts everything hums. Let me teach you a song that worms all over the earth sing. Are you ready to learn our song?"

"Yes, Grandfather!"

"WHAT WE DO DOWN HERE,
    LETS THEM LIVE UP THERE.
        WHAT WE DO AND HOW
            WE CHEW,
        HOW WE WORM,
            AND HOW WE SQUIRM,
                HOW WE WRIGGLE,
                    AND HOW WE
                        SQUIGGLE,

            LETS THEM LIVE
                UP THERE."

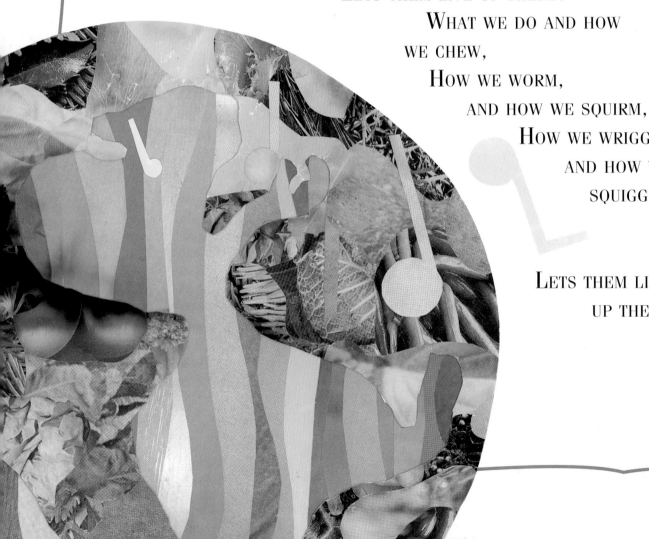

"Now you sing it, Herman."

Herman shrank. "I can't sing."

"Would you try for me?" said Grandfather.
Herman sang shyly.

"Listen to you!" Grandfather said. "You sang it!"

"I did? ... I did! Now I want
to sing it for Marguerite.
She's all alone in the
lonely orchard."

As he squirmed up, Herman sang,
and the worms in the tunnels sang with him.
Then he made up his own song.

His own song!

Herman poked up under the mushroom.

"Marguerite?"

SHHHP.

"I'm here, Herman."

"I made up a song, Marguerite, don't laugh."

"I won't laugh. Go ahead, Herman."

Herman stood straight as a stick. He turned purple from embarrassment.

"I'M HERMAN
        THE WORMIN'
AND I LIKE
        MY SQUIRMIN'
AND I LIKE
BEING CLOSE TO
        THE GROUND."

Marguerite applauded with all her feet. "Herman, it's wonderful. Sing it again!"

Herman sang again.
He sang louder.
He wiggled his head and wobbled his end.

They both rolled around laughing.

"I'M HERMAN THE WORMIN'," Herman
sang. Marguerite joined,
"And a chomp, chomp."
"AND I LIKE MY SQUIRMIN',"
"AND A CHOMP, CHOMP."

"This is fun," said Herman. "Can
we keep singing every day and
cheer up the orchard?"
"Well, Herman," said
Marguerite, "It needs..."
"...us!" Herman exclaimed.
"Yes! If we sing every day, maybe
animals will come—and bees!
Bees help the trees
make apples."

Day after day, they sang.
Then one day Marguerite said,
"Sing softly, Herman, I see two deer
hiding in the bush."

The shy deer quivered forward and
tapped. In the grass, some
beetles tapped back.

The apple trees stood a
tiny bit taller.

Next two fat frogs came.
They looked like paper bags full of wind.

They weren't shy.
They brocked right in.

"BROCK-BROCK."

"BROCKA BROCKA

BROCK-BROCK."

Under the earth,
millipedes jiggled along
with the song.

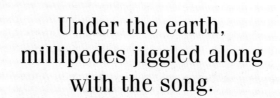

One chilly morning, Marguerite told Herman that it was time for her to change into a butterfly.

"What's a butterfly?"

"It's like a flying flower," Marguerite explained.

Amazed, Herman asked, "How can you change into something else?"

"I hang upside down in a little sack I spin."

"That's scary," Herman said. "What about the orchard, Marguerite? It will still be lonely."

"Maybe the animals will come to hear us sing in the spring, Herman."

"I hope so. Bye, Marguerite. I'll miss you," Herman said. "See you in the spring, Marguerite."

Herman headed to his tunnel and Marguerite inched toward the tree. But she got stuck between some rocks. The more she struggled, the worse it got.

"Herman!" she cried, "The rocks are crushing me! Help!"

Herman wriggled around toward Marguerite's voice. He crawled up and pushed as hard as he could, but he couldn't budge the rocks.

"Marguerite, I'll shake the whole earth if I have to. Hang on!"

Herman sped into his tunnel.
"Grandfather! The rocks are crushing Marguerite! Can we get all the worms to sing? Maybe together we can shake her free."
Herman sang and Grandfather sang too.

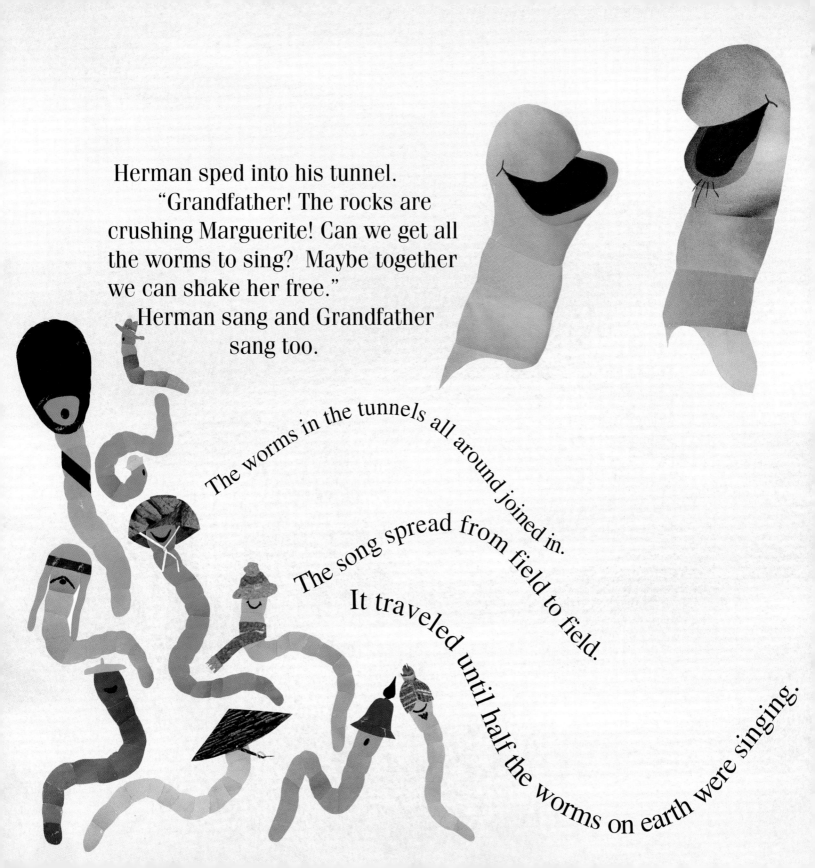

The worms in the tunnels all around joined in.
The song spread from field to field.
It traveled until half the worms on earth were singing.

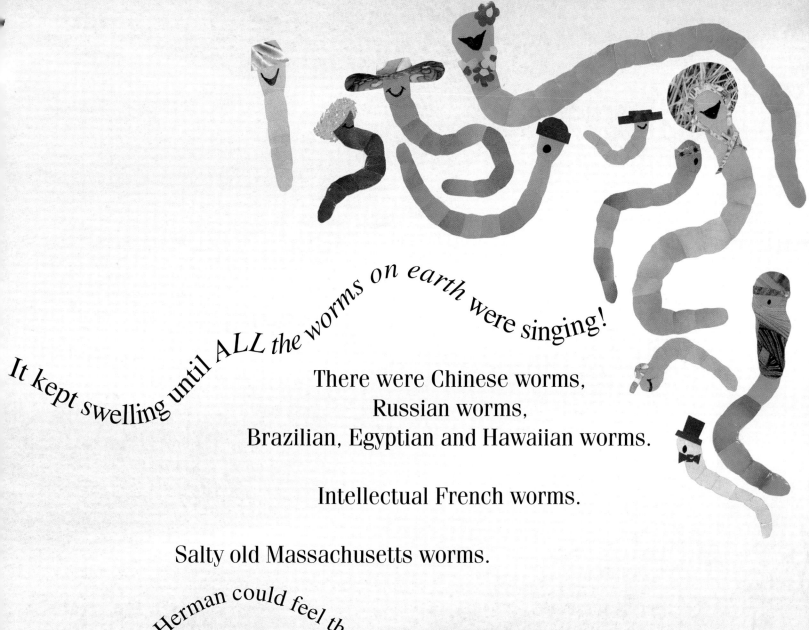

It kept swelling until *ALL the worms on earth* were singing!

There were Chinese worms,
Russian worms,
Brazilian, Egyptian and Hawaiian worms.

Intellectual French worms.

Salty old Massachusetts worms.

Herman could feel the earth trembling... It was working!

He squirmed up just as the rock pile fell apart.

"You did it!" Marguerite shouted. "Herman, you shook the earth." "Yes, with the help of a few billion friends."

Then Marguerite crawled up an apple tree. Out on the lowest branch, she spun a button of silk, glued herself to it, and hung upside down. She shed her skin and underneath was her little sack—her chrysalis.

"Bye, Marguerite!" Herman called. "We'll sing together when you're a flying flower."

Herman tunneled down below the frost line. Inside her chrysalis, Marguerite began to melt into a caterpillar soup.

Herman slept in his den all winter.

One morning, after the winter,
Marguerite's chrysalis split along the side
like a pea pod. She crawled out and hung
upside down on the branch.
    Slowly, she breathed life into her wings.
        They grew larger and larger.
            In an hour, they were twice as big.

She
    leapt
       backward
        into
         the air.

A thrill shot through her. A swirling gust tumbled her
'round and colors whirled by—blue, white, green. She
spread her wings and sang out, "I can fly!"

At that moment, Herman awoke and felt a trickle
of water. "It's spring! I hope Marguerite's
all right." He wiggled upward and poked his head
out of the earth under a soft spring mushroom.
"Marguerite. Are you here?"

"Herman!
I'm *here*,

and I can
FLY!"

Marguerite flew down and hovered
over a puddle.
"I'm a flying flower!"
Marguerite began to sing.

"I CAN SOAR. I CAN FLY.
I CAN TUMBLE WAY UP HIGH.
I CAN FLY!!"

Herman sang back,
"GO, MARGUERITE, GO!"

She sailed up into the fragrant trees.
            "Herman! The trees have
        beautiful blossoms."
    She set herself down on a blossom.
"I can taste through my feet!"
"Sweet feet," Herman laughed.
"The ground is jiggling, Marguerite. Who's coming?"
"The deer," she called.
"And the frogs… Everybody's   coming."

                    "The bees, Herman.
                        Here come the bees!"

"Hurrah for the bees!" Herman sang out.
"They came to join our song.
Let's sing!"

Herman hummed,
   rabbits drummed.
Frogs brocked,
   ants rocked.
      Bees  bumbled,
millipedes tumbled.

Turtles danced,
ladybugs pranced.
   Dragonflies glittered,
      skunks tittered.
      And the wasps were polite!

The orchard was so happy, it
lifted its limbs, opened
   its blossoms, and
danced in the breeze.

Grandfather felt the
roots of an apple tree tingle.
He came up under the mushroom,
sat a while, and listened to all the songs
blending together.
Finally, in his deep,
slow voice, he said,
"Herman, this place
has got the buzz
of life on it!"

I love thinking about
how happy the orchard is
now—full of apples, dancing
in the sun,
and all because of
Herman and Marguerite.

Digging Deeper

Worms and the earth are pretty old friends. For 700 million years, worms have been enriching the earth by making tunnels, eating leaves, and leaving castings. They are perfectly adapted to their work. Let's dig deeper to discover more about this very special animal...

THE RINGS ON AN EARTHWORM'S BODY help it wriggle forward and backward. If you watch an earthworm move, you can see the slightly pointed end goes first. This is the head. The worm also has a top side and a belly side. If you turn a worm over, it will immediately right itself.

WORMS BREATHE THROUGH THEIR SKINS much like fish and can live submerged in water for a time. They are so well adapted to life underground that if their skin dries out or they are exposed to light for a long time, they will die. When the soil gets too warm or too dry, the earthworm goes deeper to find moisture. Worms also go deeper into the earth when the earth begins to freeze, moving below the frost line.

WORMS DON'T HAVE EARS but they can feel vibrations. Charles Darwin, the naturalist, tried playing on a whistle for some worms, but they didn't respond. Then he put worms in a flowerpot on his piano and began to play, and they seemed to get excited about the C in the treble clef!

Worms don't need eyes because they live and work in the dark earth.

The earthworm is like us in that its body uses blood to deliver food and oxygen to its muscles and organs. Unlike us, however, a worm has five pairs of hearts and can grow a new head or tail if it loses one.

The earthworm has many enemies: Birds, lizards, and snakes are among them. But humans are the greatest foe of the worm. When we spray insecticides on the land, the rain washes the sprays into the soil, and the poison can kill worms by the millions.

An acre of soil may be home to a million earthworms. Their burrowing mixes and sifts the soil, breaks up clods of dirt, and buries stones. They carry leaves down and bring nutrients and humus to the top. Earthworms work hard!

Hooray for the worm, the earth's best friend!

Worms aren't the only creatures who help the earth. Honeybees and butterflies get their food, called nectar, from flowers. While they gather the nectar, pollen collects on the bees' furry bodies and the butterflies' sticky feet. As the bees and butterflies fly to different flowers, the pollen on their bodies rubs off on other flowers. Pollen has to move from one flower to another for fruit to grow. This is called pollenation.

All creatures have to work together and be friends of the earth. Worms and caterpillars help by recycling —they eat plant matter, turning it into waste that then fertilizes the soil. Bees and butterflies help plants grow by moving pollen among all the flowers. Turn the page and find out how you can be a friend to the earth too...

Flying Higher

As Herman's grandfather says, "everyone has a gift, and when we use our gifts, everything hums." When Herman and Marguerite work and sing together, the whole orchard comes to life. You can find many ways to help the earth and play a part in our world, and you can have fun at the same time! For starters, you can try the ideas on this page. Then, spread your wings and be creative in your world.

RECYCLING

Worms are natural recyclers! If your family or a neighbor has a compost pile, they can show you how worms help recycle leaves, food leftovers, and grass clippings into rich new soil. You can help the earth, too, by recycling used newspapers, aluminum cans, glass bottles, and plastic jugs.

CUT-PAPER COLLAGES

Artist Laura O'Callahan created the pictures in this book by cutting up colored pictures from old magazines and gluing the pieces together to form "collages." Find some old magazines or colored paper, some scissors, some glue, and a sheet of blank paper and make your own collages. Try many different colors and interesting shapes. You are also recycling as you make a collage, turning old papers into a brand new piece of art.

WORM FOOD

Herman likes to eat leaves, vegetables, bits of grass cuttings—all sorts of organic matter. If you have a worm bin, you can find out which foods worms like best by giving them little pieces of celery leaves, carrot tops, or cabbage leaves. They usually prefer food that is a few days old—not fresh like we do.

BUTTERFLY FOOD

When Marguerite came out of her chrysalis, she was a butterfly. If you have a garden or a few outdoor flower pots, you can plant black-eyed Susan, azalea, or lantana to attract butterflies. They love the bright colors and the sweet nectar in the flowers.